the BAD GUYS

in

DAWN OF THE
UNDERLORD

PLANET :(

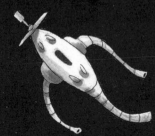

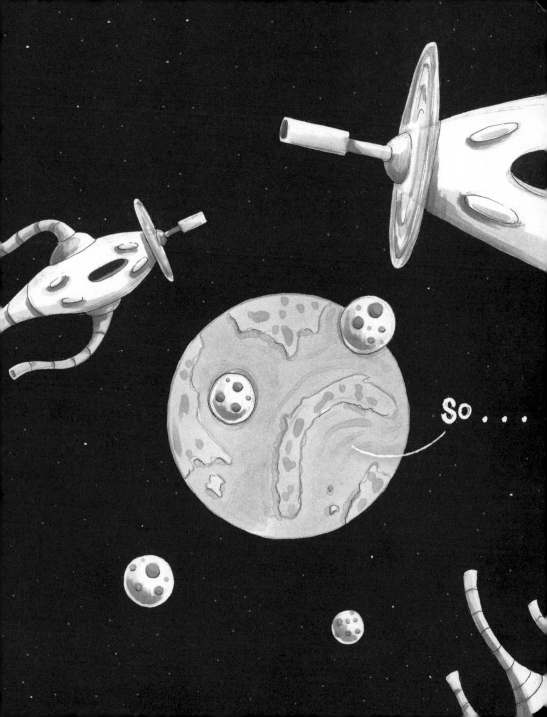

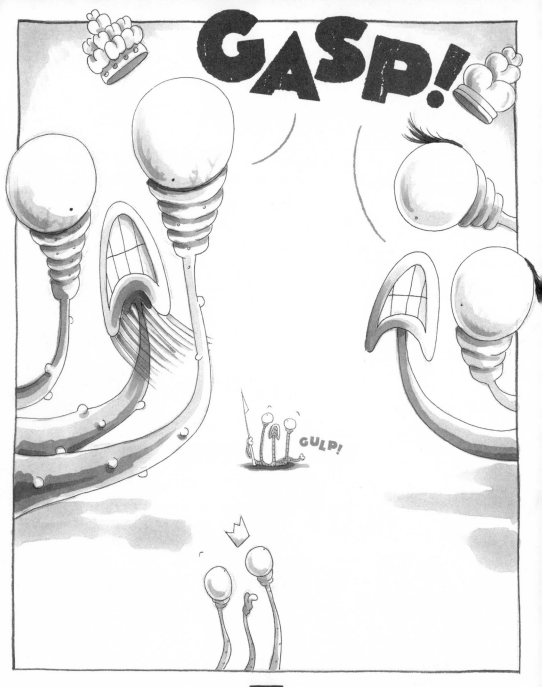

WHAT ABOUT IT?!

Well, remember how
before I left, you were all like,

**"DON'T USE THOSE CANNONS!
THEY'RE, LIKE, TOTALLY WHACK AND
DON'T WORK PROPERLY AND STUFF!"**

. . . or something.
Well, guess what?

STOP!

AND FURTHERMORE, I SAT YOU DOWN, LOOKED YOU IN THE EYE, AND SAID VERY CLEARLY— "IF YOU REMEMBER **ONE THING**, REMEMBER THIS: **WHATEVER YOU DO, DON'T FIRE THOSE CANNONS** OR USE **ANY** OF THE **TIME-TRAVEL EQUIPMENT!** BECAUSE IF YOU **DO**, YOU'LL START A **CHAIN REACTION** THAT WILL **OBLITERATE OUR UNIVERSE!** EVERY LIVING CREATURE IN EVERY SINGLE GALAXY WILL DIE A **HORRIBLE, HORRIBLE** DEATH."

THAT
IS WHAT I SAID.

... AND IF **ONE** TINY CREATURE ATTEMPTED TO **USE** THAT TERRIBLE POWER, THEN THE **ENTIRE UNIVERSE** WOULD BE ...

PLANET EARTH

...DOOMED.

· CHAPTER 1 ·
HERO HQ

Hiiiiiii, everyone!

This is **TIFFANY FLUFFIT**

—A.K.A. **T-FLUFF**—

bringing you the hottest

new show on the planet:

HANGIN' with the HEROES!

SHADOW SQUAD G

That's right! I'll be taking you **INSIDE** their not-so-secret **HEADQUARTERS.**

HERO HQ LIVE

And who better to show us around than everybody's **FAVORITE** team member . . .

In fact, here's my pops! Hey, **PAPA!** Say hello to the BIGGEST LIVE AUDIENCE in HISTORY!

You're wasting too much money on that burrito chef, **PEPE.** Your spending is totally out of control. You have a **PROBLEM** and you need—

HAHAHAHA! Papa is old, so he *doesn't know what he's saying.* But man, I love him, you know?

But . . . how DID you guys **AFFORD** all this? You don't get paid for being heroes.

No, but I *diversify*. Once we **CLEANED UP THE PLANET,** there were no more bad guys to fight, so I decided to *follow my dreams*. I took all the **LOVE** the world has given me . . .

. . . and started my own **RECORD LABEL.** As you know, my debut single was **#1** on the global charts for an entire year, and that allowed me to really spread my fins.

I'LL BITE YO BUTT

QUADRUPLE PLATINUM

I now have my own **FASHION LABEL** . . .

Edgy . . .

I own a **BASKETBALL TEAM** . . .

Go, Mayhem!

I have the **THIRD-HIGHEST RATED SHOW** on the Cooking Network . . .

Eww.

And my new **FRAGRANCE** is breaking hearts across the nation.

STANK

Oh my . . . gak!

But it's as a **MUSIC PRODUCER** that I've really found my *sweet spot*. And I've just signed a new band that is **SMOKIN' HOT**. Check *this* . . .

RECORDING

STUDIO 2

Well, there just aren't as many wrongs to right these days. The world seems pretty chill, so I've decided to chill out for a bit, too.

For a change.

You know, I get told I look like you . . .

Oh really?

I *KNOW!* I don't see it, because I'm a *cat* and you're . . . like . . . a fox. We're, like, *totally* different, really.

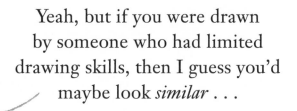

Yeah, but if you were drawn by someone who had limited drawing skills, then I guess you'd maybe look *similar* . . .

Just sayin'.

FIRE?!

What's going on?!

Aha! Well, it's not all
rock n roll around here, *chica*.
We like to mix it up!
It's time to get your
SCIENCE on,
baby . . .

Oooh! What *peaceful* music.

It helps **CLEAR THE MIND** and brings you back in touch with yourself.

I used to be a **MASTER OF DISGUISE.** But once we cleared the world of bad vibes, I lost interest in disguising myself. I realized I needed to turn *inward* . . .

... and discover who I really am.

He's a **SHARK.**

By which I mean, who I am on the *inside* ...

Oh man. He's had all of us on the *inside*, at one time or another. He'll eat **ANYTHING.**

My friend, I must tell you—
with love—that it would make
me *happy* if you *stopped talking*
and *moved onward*, like the
majestic Amazon River cutting
through the jungle . . .

I think that's code
for "go away."
Am I right?

Go in peace.

That dude has *changed*, you know? I'm not sure how I feel about it.

REV! REV! REV!

Oh!
I DON'T BELIEVE IT!
IS THAT **HIM?!**

It's HIM alright!
He needs no introduction . . .
but I'll give him one anyway.
IN THIS CORNER!
THE **BADDEST DUDE**
ON THE PLANET, THE UNOFFICIAL
LEADER OF THE FREE WORLD
BECAUSE HE'S JUST *SO* POPULAR . . .

IT'S . . .

DRIIIIIIIIIIIIIIIIIIIIIIIIIIIIIFT . . .

YES HE DID

VOTE ①

. . . oh, you know who it is.

'Sup?

WINK!

I've gotta hand it to him. Those entrances are getting pretty good.

And you're the most **POWERFUL** guy we've ever seen!

Well, now, I'll have to stop you there. Don't *want* to. But I will. If it's **POWER** you're looking for . . . one of us is kind of **OFF-THE-CHARTS** in that department.

You're talking about **MR. SNAKE,** aren't you?

Let me show you something *amazing* . . .

And hold on to your hat!

KNOCK! KNOCKITTY KNOCK KNOCK!

Are you sure about this?

I was thinking of **SKIPPING** this part of the tour, Wolfie. You know how he gets.

Nonsense. He'll be delighted to—

Yeah.

We're something, alright.

ALONE TIME

OK.
Back to it.

Bored of this room.
Too much POWER for
one little room.
Let's look
BEYOND . . .

And there they are.
Knuckleheads. Everywhere
I look, *knuckleheads*.

I have to look a little farther . . .

Oh man.
There has to be
more than *this*.

THERE IS MORE!

Where?! Where is there more?
And what does that mean?
More of *WHAT?!*

USE YOUR POWER!
PUSH THROUGH,
YOU'LL SEE!

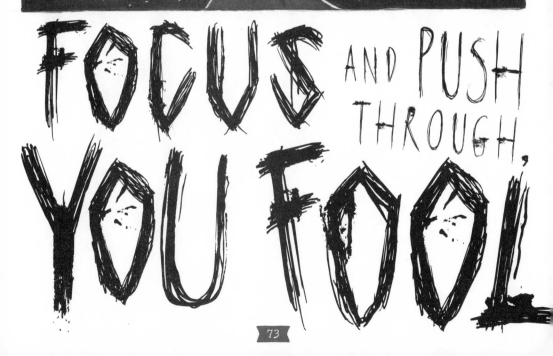

GUHRRRRRRRRRGH!

OK, I've got the solar system . . . a lot of space . . . yeah, just more of the same old stuff, dude . . .

FOCUS AND PUSH THROUGH YOU FOOL!

OK. That's new. I'll give you that.

YOU'VE DONE IT.

I'VE WAITED SO LONG, SO MANY MILLIONS OF YEARS.

Oh really?
So . . . what am I looking
at here, exactly?

Well, duh. But a door to *what?*
And why is it floating in that . . .
I want to say "hole in the universe"?
Yep, I'm going to say,
"WHY IS IT FLOATING IN THAT HOLE IN THE UNIVERSE?"

DOMINATION OF ALL THINGS

Ohhh, *that.*
Look, I'm intrigued, but . . .

OPEN THE DOOR

If you go all the way back to my idea about **TURNING GOOD . . .** well, that led to **FIGHTING ZOMBIE KITTENS** and **ALIENS** and **DINOSAURS** and even a **GIANT VERSION OF ME** at one point, didn't it?

Yeah, yeah, I know. I was there. Lots happened. Basically, if our life was a **SERIES,** it would be like **10 EPISODES** worth of stuff.

So, what's your point?

Well, since then, you've kind of been spending a lot of time **ALONE.** Which, for a guy who everyone loves, is a bit . . . surprising.

I like alone time.

You haven't left that room since *September.*

Nope.

You are! You told me the other day. You said, *"I'm worried about Snake."*

I didn't.
I said . . . uh . . .
"Slime, curried . . . without steak."
Yeah. I was ordering not-great, spicy vegetarian food and you misunderstood.
Yeah.

· CHAPTER 3 ·
A BAD FEELING

It ain't a **POOL PARTY** 'til I drop my bomb, baby!

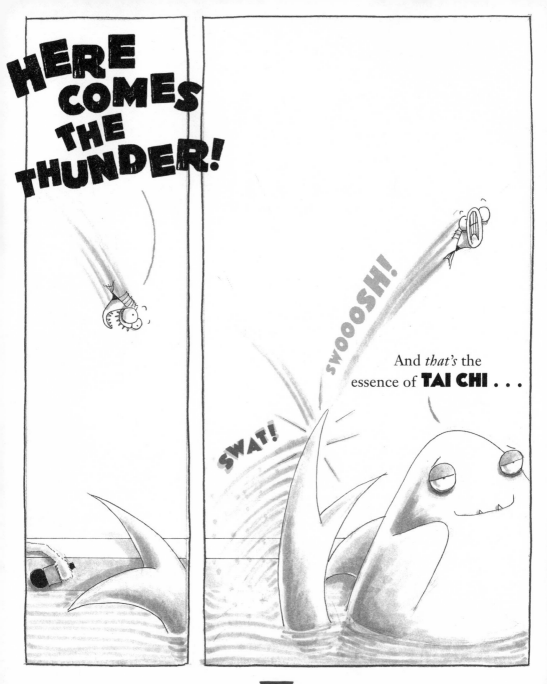

SHUNK!

AND...

...fluid movement.
At **ONE** with your
surroundings.

SPLASH!

. . . You're welcome!

Whoa.

You should go pro.

GRIIIIIND!
THUNKA-VOOOSH!

I've thought about it.

But who needs that kind of pressure?

You sure about this?
I tend to annoy him . . .

It'll be great. I think
he just needs a little
guidance . . .

· CHAPTER 4 ·
KNOCKITTY KNOCK KNOCK

So, you're talking about what? DOMINATION over the **ENTIRE UNIVERSE?**

HAHAHAHAHAHA, YOUR UNIVERSE IS PUNY. THINK OF IT AS A CRUMMY TRUCK STOP ON AN ENDLESS HIGHWAY THAT LEADS TO AN INFINITE CITY OF MAGNIFICENCE!

OK, you've lost me.
I'm not ashamed to say it.

DID YOU REALLY THINK YOUR UNIVERSE WAS **THE ONLY ONE?**

Well, yep. I kind of did, yeah.

IT IS MERELY **ANOTHER LAYER** OF AN INFINITE **MULTIVERSE!** UNIVERSE UPON UNIVERSE **LAYERED** UPON EACH OTHER, **SEPARATED ONLY** BY

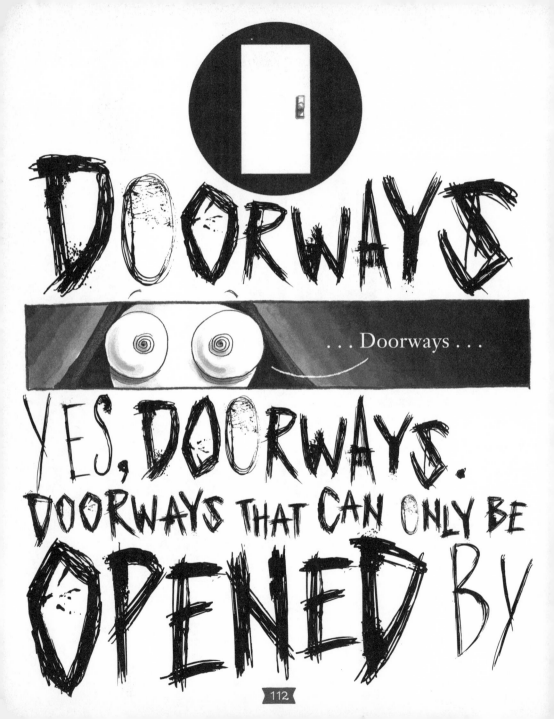

DOORWAYS

. . . Doorways . . .

YES, DOORWAYS.
DOORWAYS THAT CAN ONLY BE
OPENED BY

Come again?

YOU HEARD ME, SERPENT. IT'S TIME TO FULFILL YOUR DESTINY.

My...

YOUR ENTIRE LIFE YOU'VE BEEN MISUNDERSTOOD, HATED, AND FEARED.

Well, yes, but then Wolf . . .

YOUR ENTIRE LIFE YOU'VE FELT DESTINED FOR SOMETHING MORE.

Yeah, but . . .

YOU'VE BEEN HATED AND FEARED BECAUSE YOU JUST CAN'T HIDE YOUR TRUE NATURE

Oh, so this is the part where you call me a **MEAN LITTLE SNAKE**, is it?

· CHAPTER 5 ·
PARTY'S OVER

GASP!

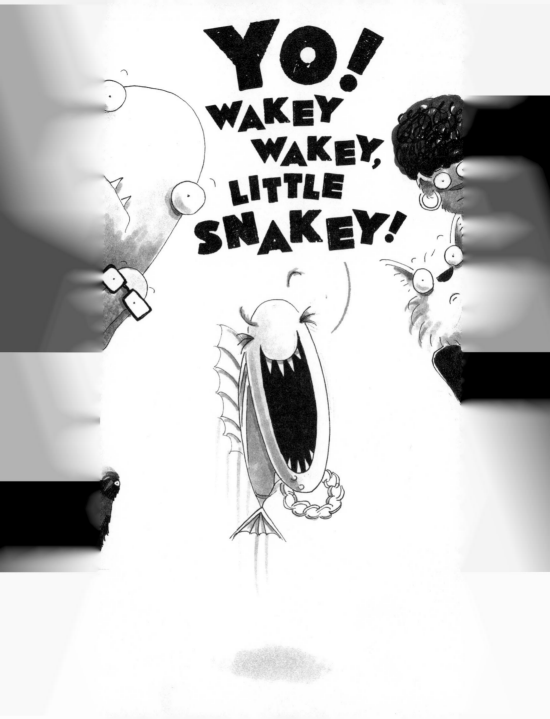

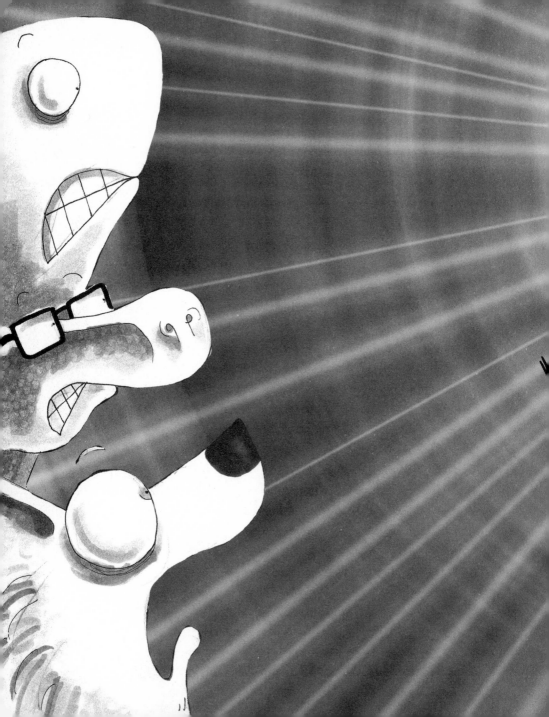

· CHAPTER 6 ·
BAD INFLUENCE

Sure is, buddy.
It's time to play

OUTSIDE

for a bit.
That's enough alone time,
I think . . .

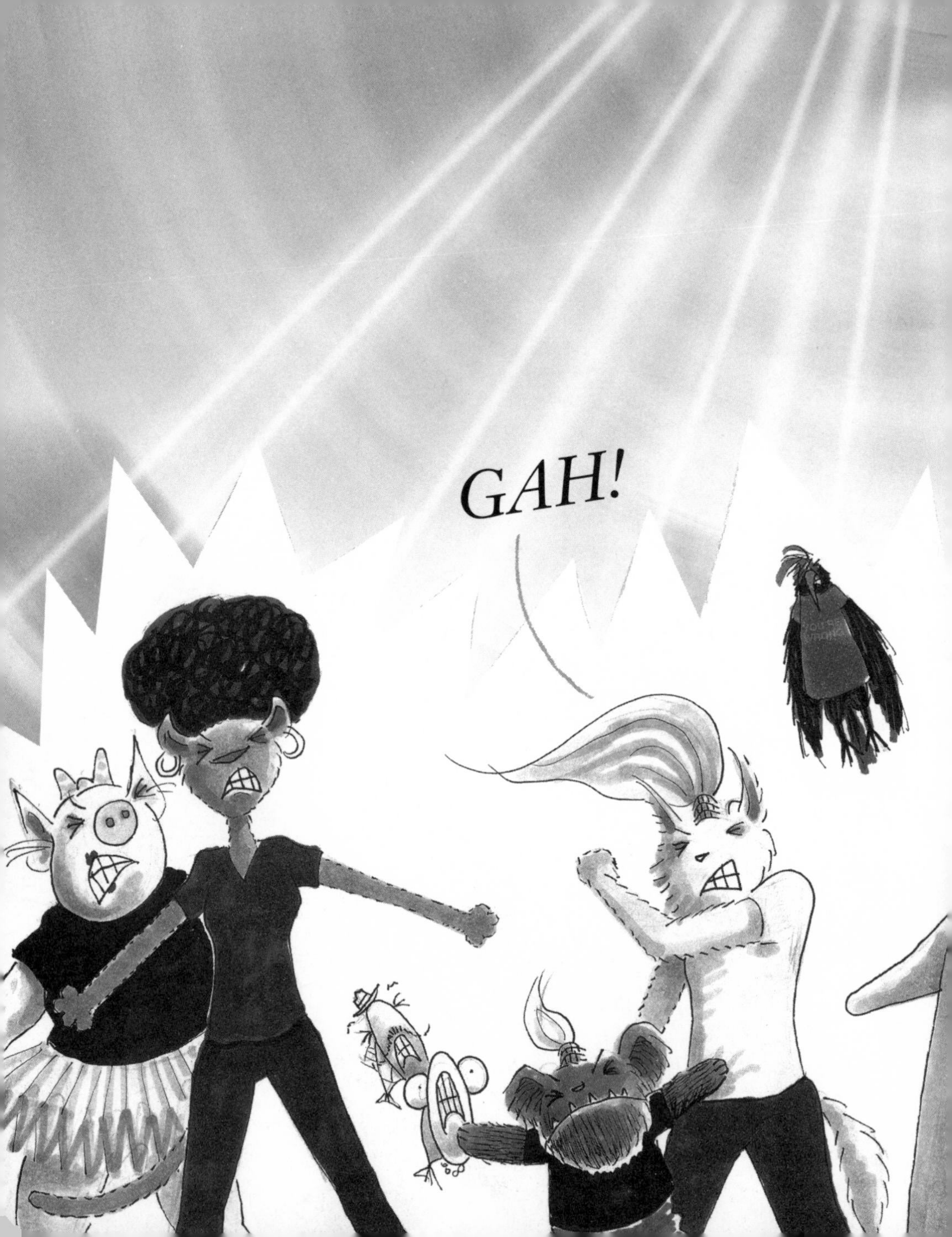
GAH!

If you're just joining us at home, my little story about Hero HQ has taken on an unexpected—potentially *award-winning*—turn . . .

· CHAPTER 7 ·
UNDERLORD

ARE YOU READY, DARK LORD OF SERPENTS?

Ooooh . . . I DO like the sound of *that.*

AND WHAT OF THE RUMOR OF THE ONE?

I DON'T LISTEN TO RUMORS AND NEITHER SHOULD YOU.

DARK LORD OF SERPENTS, IT IS TIME.